SOMEBODY LOVES YOU, MR. HATCH

By Eileen Spinelli

Pictures by Paul Yalowitz

Bradbury Press/New York

Collier Macmillan Canada/Toronto

Maxwell Macmillan International Publishing Group
New York/Oxford/Singapore/Sydney

WITHDRAWN
Lakewood Memorial Library
Lakewood, New York 14750

A NOTE ON THE ART

The illustrations in this book were first drawn with ebony pencil on bristol plate paper and then colored over with Derwent color pencils. Because the artist is right-handed, he starts drawing on the left side of the paper and moves to the right so that the picture won't smudge. The paper is very smooth, and only the artist knows where that mysterious texture comes from. The illustrations were color-separated and reproduced using four-color process.

Text copyright © 1991 by Eileen Spinelli
Illustrations copyright © 1991 by Paul Yalowitz

All rights reserved. No part of this book may be reproduced or transmitted in any form or by any means, electronic or mechanical, including photocopying, recording, or by any information storage and retrieval system, without permission in writing from the Publisher.

Bradbury Press
Macmillan Publishing Company
866 Third Avenue
New York, NY 10022

Collier Macmillan Canada, Inc.
1200 Eglinton Avenue East
Suite 200
Don Mills, Ontario M3C 3N1

First American edition
Printed and bound in Hong Kong
by South China Printing Company (1988) Ltd.
10 9 8 7 6 5 4 3 2 1

The text of this book is set in Leawood Book.
Book design by Christy Hale and Cathy Bobak

Library of Congress Cataloging-in-Publication Data
Spinelli, Eileen.
   Somebody loves you, Mr. Hatch / by Eileen Spinelli ; illustrated by
Paul Yalowitz.— 1st American ed.
      p.   cm.
   Summary: An anonymous valentine changes the life of the unsociable
Mr. Hatch, turning him into a laughing friend who helps and appreciates all his neighbors.
   ISBN 0-02-786015-9
   [1. Neighborliness—Fiction.]   I. Yalowitz, Paul, ill.
II. Title.
PZ7.S7566So   1992
[E]—dc20   90-33016

To my parents
and to my three sisters,
Tina, Donna, and Jo
—E.S.

To that little bit of Mr. Hatch
in all of us
—P.Y.

9/92 Obl Morrow Mae millan 13.95

Mr. Hatch was tall and thin and he did not smile.
  Every morning at 6:30 sharp he would leave his brick house and walk eight blocks to the shoelace factory where he worked.
  At lunchtime he would sit alone in a corner, eat his cheese and mustard sandwich, and drink a cup of coffee. Sometimes he brought a prune for dessert.

Lakewood Memorial Library
Lakewood, New York 14750

After work he would make two stops:

at the newsstand
to get the paper,

and at the grocery store
to buy a fresh turkey wing
for his supper.

After supper he read the paper, took a shower, and went to bed early.
 "He keeps to himself." That is what everyone said about Mr. Hatch.

One Saturday, when Mr. Hatch stepped onto the porch with his dustpan and broom, he got a surprise—a package wrapped in brown paper.

He had never spoken to the postman before. "Thank you, Mr. Goober," he said.

Mr. Goober smiled. "You're welcome. I always enjoy delivering packages."

Mr. Hatch tore the brown paper off. Inside was a white box, which he opened to find another box. This one was heart-shaped— all satiny red with a pink bow on top. It was filled with candy. Something fluttered to the porch floor. It was a little white card. He picked it up. It said, "Somebody loves you."

Only then did he remember that this was Valentine's Day.

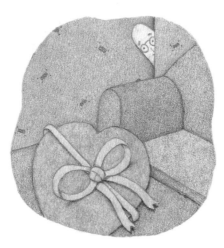

Mr. Hatch wondered and wondered. "Now who would send this to me?" He was all alone. He had no friends. And yet someone—*someone*—had sent him a valentine. Who?...Who?...

He put the box on the coffee table and tried to do some dusting, but every time he left the room he had to keep peeking to see if the box was still there.

He dusted and dusted, and the dustcloth seemed to whisper: "Somebody loves you....Somebody loves you...." At last he flung the dustcloth away and exclaimed, "Why, I've got a secret admirer!"

And then he did something he had never done before: He laughed. He laughed and danced and clapped his hands. And then he took a piece of candy from the box and ate it.

Mr. Hatch changed his shirt and found some old aftershave in the bottom drawer. He splashed it on his face. He picked out a yellow tie with blue polka dots and put it on.

And then he went for a walk. "Maybe," he thought, "I will meet the person who sent me the candy."

Of course no one had ever seen Mr. Hatch wearing a tie, or smelling of aftershave, or smiling. So he got a lot of attention.

Mrs. Weed tripped over her dog.

Mr. Dunwoody nearly fell off his ladder.

And little Tina Finn spilled all the toys out of her wagon.

Mr. Hatch waved hello to them all.

On Monday it was back to work. At lunchtime Mr. Hatch sat in the middle of the cafeteria. He spoke to everyone and passed out chocolates from his heart box.

On the way home, as usual, he stopped at the newsstand. Mr. Smith handed him the usual newspaper. "I think I'll have a pack of mints," said Mr. Hatch, not as usual.

Mr. Smith was shocked. "Was that you speaking, Mr. Hatch?"

"Indeed it was," said Mr. Hatch. "I said I would also like a pack of mints. And if you don't mind my saying so, Mr. Smith, you don't look very well today."

Mr. Smith recovered from his shock to reply, "You're right. I don't feel very well. I have a cold. I was supposed to go to the doctor's this afternoon, but the stand has been so busy I haven't had the time."

Mr. Hatch smiled. "Why, I'd be happy to watch the stand for you while you go."

Mr. Smith could hardly believe his ears. "You would?"

"Certainly. Just show me what to do."

And so Mr. Hatch ran the newsstand for an hour. He wondered if any of the women who stopped to buy a paper, or a magazine, or a candy bar, had sent him the mysterious valentine.

When Mr. Smith returned, Mr. Hatch made his usual stop at the grocery store. "I'm a little tired of turkey wings," he told Mr. Todd. "I think I'll have a nice fresh slice of ham."

Mr. Todd weighed the meat and wrapped it. "You look worried," said Mr. Hatch.

"I am," said Mr. Todd. "My little girl is late. She hasn't come home from school yet, and I can't leave the store to look for her until my wife arrives."

"Goodness! Why didn't you say so?" said Mr. Hatch. "I will go look for her."

And so he walked to school and found little Melanie Todd by the swings and brought her home.

"Thank you, thank you," said the grocer.

"Anytime," said Mr. Hatch.

After supper Mr. Hatch did not bother to read the paper. He decided to bake brownies instead. It would be nice to have brownies to share the next day with the people at the shoelace factory.

As he baked, the warm chocolate smell of brownies floated through the neighborhood. Children gathered round Mr. Hatch's house, sniffing the air.

"Well, I suppose the factory can wait," said Mr. Hatch as he looked out the window. And he brought out two platefuls.

"Now what are brownies without lemonade?" he said, and he stirred up a nice cold pitcher.

When the parents came to gather their children, they had some brownies too. It turned out to be a picnic in Mr. Hatch's backyard. He dusted off an old harmonica and played songs he remembered from his boyhood.

Everyone danced.

And so the days and weeks went by. When Mr. Hatch wasn't smiling, he was laughing. And when he wasn't laughing he was helping someone. And when he wasn't helping someone, he was having a party in his yard or on his porch.

He seemed to have forgotten about finding the person who sent him the valentine.

Then one afternoon Mr. Goober, the postman, came to his door. His face was very serious. "Come in, Mr. Goober," said Mr. Hatch. "You look upset."

"I am upset," he said. "I made a mistake some time ago. My supervisor is very angry with me. Do you…do you…"

"Yes, Mr. Goober? What is it?"

"Do you recall the package I delivered to you? On Valentine's Day, I think it was."

"Yes, I believe so," replied Mr. Hatch, beginning to feel a little uneasy.

"I don't suppose you still have it," said Mr. Goober sadly.

"As a matter of fact," said Mr. Hatch, "I still have the box. The candy is gone, though. Why do you ask?"

The postman took a deep breath. "I'm afraid I delivered it to the wrong address. It was supposed to go to another house."

Mr. Hatch recalled tearing off the brown paper. It had never occured to him to look at the address. He fetched the heart-shaped box and the pink bow and gave them to the postman. "I do hope your supervisor won't be too angry with you now."

The postman was heading down the sidewalk when Mr. Hatch called from his porch. "Mr. Goober, I forgot something!" He gave the postman the little white card.

Alone in his living room, Mr. Hatch sighed. "Nobody loved me after all." Then he read the paper, took his shower, and went to bed early.

The next morning at 6:30 sharp, Mr. Hatch left his brick house and walked eight blocks to the shoelace factory. At lunchtime he sat in the corner by himself, ate his cheese and mustard sandwich, and drank a cup of coffee.

After work he stopped at the
newsstand for his paper,
but he did not speak to Mr. Smith.

And when he ordered
his turkey wing from Mr. Todd,
he did not smile.

Nor did he pat little Melanie Todd
on the head or bake brownies or have
picnics or parties or play his old
harmonica anymore.

Everyone whispered, "What is wrong with Mr. Hatch?"
Mr. Goober, the postman, told them.

"We love Mr. Hatch," insisted Mr. and Mrs. Dunwoody. "He gave us flowers for our garden. He helped to mend our back fence."

Mrs. Weed nodded. "I love him too. He saved his bones for my dog Ruffy." Ruffy barked—she loved Mr. Hatch too.

Mr. Smith told everyone how Mr. Hatch had watched his newsstand so he could visit the doctor. And Mr. Todd told everyone how Mr. Hatch had found his little girl.

All the children in the neighborhood remembered Mr. Hatch's wonderful brownies and lemonade. And most of all his laughter.

"Poor Mr. Hatch," they said. "What can we do?"

Then Mr. Goober announced, "I have an idea."

Lakewood Memorial Library
Lakewood, New York 14750

On Saturday morning Mr. Hatch woke to a bright and sunny day. He put on his old overalls and went out to the porch with his dustpan and broom.

He couldn't believe his eyes. All over the porch were red and white hearts and pink bows. There were boxes of candy on the chairs and yellow streamers flowing from the ceiling. And sticking up out of his mailbox was a shining silver harmonica.

The front yard was filled with people. Happy smiling people. They were holding up a huge sign with hand-painted letters. It said:

EVERYBODY LOVES MR. HATCH

Mr. Hatch dabbed at a tear with his handkerchief.
"I do believe"— he sniffed —"somebody loves me after all."

And then he smiled.   And then he laughed.
And then he hurried down to be with his friends.

3 2005 0128999 3

Lakewood, New York 14750

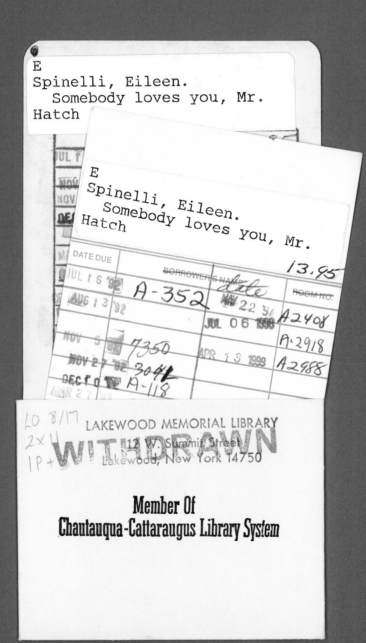

E
Spinelli, Eileen.
  Somebody loves you, Mr.
Hatch

E
Spinelli, Eileen.
  Somebody loves you, Mr.
Hatch

13.95

DATE DUE	BORROWER'S NAME	ROOM NO.
JUL 16 '92	A-352	date
AUG 13 '92		MAY 22 3| A-2408
	JUL 06 1998	
NOV 5	7350	A-2918
NOV 27 '92	3041	APR 13 1999 A-2988
DEC 0	A-118	
MAR 27		

LO 8/17 LAKEWOOD MEMORIAL LIBRARY
2x   12 W. Summit Street
IP+   WITHDRAWN Lakewood, New York 14750

Member Of
Chautauqua-Cattaraugus Library System